K

W9-AAV-460

Milton, My Father's Dog

Eric Copeland

Tundra Books

For Fraser and his mother — who endured and enjoyed a dog's life

Published in Canada by Tundra Books, Montreal, Quebec H3Z 2N2

Published in the United States by Tundra Books of Northern New York, Plattsburgh, N.Y. 12901

Library of Congress Catalog Number: 93-61795

Canadian Cataloging in Publication Data:
Copeland, Eric, 1939-
    Milton, My Father's Dog

ISBN 0-88776-339-1

    I. Title

PS8555.O5926M9 1994   jC813'.54   C94-900053-1
PZ10.3.C66M9 1994

The publisher has applied funds from its Canada Council block grant for 1994 toward the editing and production of this book.

Design by Kenneth King

Printed in Canada by D.W. Friesen Ltd.

I should never have let them go without me. But I had wanted a puppy for such a long time.

So that Saturday morning when Mom looked up from the newspaper over breakfast and said: "They have puppies for sale out at the Harris farm. Why don't we get one for Fraser?" I did not dare say: "Wait for me to go with you."

If they didn't go then, it might be months, years — maybe never — before they got around to the subject again.

I couldn't go. It was playoff time and nobody on our team missed a playoff game.

Anyway it was hard to imagine a puppy I wouldn't like. I'd thought so often of how I'd train it to obey, to heel, to sit, to fetch, to wait at the side of the rink or field and watch our games.

What a mistake!

We won the game, even though I did not play my best hockey. I was thinking too much about my parents, too worried they might not like any of the puppies and come back without one.

After the game I waited for what seemed like an hour outside the arena. The other players had been picked up or had gone home on their own. I kept telling myself that the longer my parents took, the more likely they'd have bought a puppy. They'd have to get papers and directions on how to take care of it and all that.

At last their car arrived. I ran toward it, lugging my hockey gear. I saw Mom smiling in the front seat and a head, a dog's head, in the back window.

Mom turned and opened the back door.

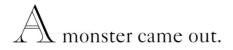A monster came out.

It ran straight for me. I had to use my hockey stick to keep from being knocked down. It put its paws on my shoulders and licked my face as if it were washing it in order to eat me.

My father got out of the car laughing and coaxed the monster into the back seat. I got in beside it.

It was all over me. I put one hand up to stop the licking and the other to take hair out of my mouth. My sweater was wet from drool and mud. The hair, fur, wool or whatever covered the monster was filthy and his breath smelled of rotten fish.

Dad turned, excited. "I always wanted an English sheep dog."

My mother smiled at me, too. "Well, Fraser," she said, "what do you think of your new dog?"

"I thought you were getting a *puppy*!" I cried.

"He's only a year old," my father said.

My parents had never got to the Harris farm.

They had seen Milton — that was the monster's name — chained to a tree, with cats teasing him, circling just beyond his reach. My father stopped the car. Maybe the owners would like to sell him. They did. Which didn't surprise me.

He had come at the bargain price of fifty dollars because his pedigree papers were lost. He should have been lost with them, I thought.

Once home, my father handed me the chain. "Here, Fraser, take him for a walk."

I might as well have tried to hold back a bull. He pulled so hard I had to let go the leash or be dragged along the ground. As soon as he got free, he'd go a short distance, then return, wagging his rear. Milton didn't have a tail.

"He's a very playful dog," my father said, when I got home, exhausted.

Milton had to be sheared, bathed and de-fleaed as soon as possible to get rid of any other creatures living under his coat. When the breeder removed six to eight inches of hair, Milton was reduced to half his size.

A fringe was left over his eyes. He had been named after the blind poet for good reason. "Don't laugh," the breeder said. "These dogs have very sensitive eyes."

Then to the vet for shots. As soon as Milton entered, everyone in the waiting room hugged their animals closer. In the corner a big beautiful Bernese mountain dog sat alone on a chair like a throne.

Milton made straight for her, slipping and sliding on the tile floor. My father used all his strength to hold him back. The Bernese looked down with queenly disdain.

Later, in telling my mother about it, my father said proudly: "Milton has taste. He went after the classiest dog there."

Whenever we went out, Milton was kept in the basement, until one day he escaped and went wild.

Milton met us at the door with the shreds of a Christmas cracker in his mouth. My toys — pieces of a board game, plastic tanks and figures from Star Wars — led us upstairs, a trail of destruction. My room looked as if Star Wars had been fought there.

"This dog has to go!" I screamed.

And go he went. But not very far or very fast. "Why don't you build Milton his own house, out in the back?" my mother suggested. It took a winter to build.

I watched, carried wood or handed Dad nails as the dog house went up in the garage.

When it was finished, it was so big and so heavy we couldn't move it through the gate or over the hedge to get it to the back yard. A neighbor helped, but even then the three of us had to carry the roof separately.

My father had fussed so much over the dog house you'd think he was going to live in it himself and he almost did, because...

Milton refused to go into it.

Even though it was beautiful. The roof and walls were made of two-by-four studs and covered on the outside with wafer board and fully insulated. The floor was of plywood and the building sat on a foundation of bricks. As the final artistic touch, Mom contributed a piece of carpeting to hang over the entrance and break the wind.

But even food could not coax Milton to go inside. So Dad decided to crawl into it himself to demonstrate. Mom and I watched from the kitchen window, sick with laughter, wondering if Dad would get stuck in the entrance.

Finally, Dad gave up. Later as we watched from the window we saw Milton decide to try it out. He crawled on his belly *under* the carpet, careful not to touch it.

"He doesn't want to disturb it," my father said.

The next morning the carpet lay in shreds.

Milton was asleep in his house — not lying on his stomach or his side the way any normal dog sleeps, but upside down with his legs in the air and his head out the doorway.

Having his own house didn't mean that Milton was not allowed into ours. Whenever Mom or Dad was home, there was Milton asking to be patted, begging food — or stealing it.

It didn't seem to bother Mom that a half pound of butter could disappear off the kitchen table.

When she pared turnips, carrots or celery for soup, Milton got as much as the pot. As for cookies, he ate more than I did.

"He eats just like a person," my father said.

The only kind of person Milton could have been was a clown.

He certainly made everyone laugh.

At the hockey rink my teammates thought he was hilarious. He wanted to play with us. But when he tried to run, he slid. When he tried to stop, he slid. He ended up walking very gingerly, his large black nose pushed down and forward on the ice like an extra foot.

In summer my friends liked to race Milton across the fields. They had to keep well ahead of him. If he caught up, he did not run by them. He knocked them down and ran *over* them.

And my parents certainly treated Milton as if he were human. They never bought ice cream without a cone for Milton. Even I had to admit he was funny.

Evenings he was allowed into the house to watch TV with us. He seemed to know when the commercials came on. It was time for him to beg for a scratch or a rub.

"He's so intelligent!" my father said.

Time solves many problems, my mother liked to say, and that's what solved the Milton problem for me.

I was growing bigger. Milton wasn't. He never learned to heel, but I was gradually able to control him on a strong leather leash. He no longer pulled me down.

But the big change came the day he tried to wrestle me to the ground, and I pinned him down instead. He lay quite still while I rested my head on top of him. He felt soft and warm as a pillow. He waited patiently until I let him get up.

That night I told my father: "I guess Milton's an okay dog."

"Just what I've always said," my father answered.